Up in the gullery things have been very peaceful lately. I'\
chilled, you know? A chilled gull if ever there was one.

This might have something to do with the time of year of course. Spring is lovely
here in Cornwall. Its beginning to get warmer, the evenings are getting longer, the
gullery isn't as windy and these are things that make all of us, gulls and people,
love the springtime.

Of course it's good that the Easter holiday is over. Easter is the first time each year when the ghastly Trumpers come down from Bristol to stay in their holiday cottage, and that is always horrid. But between Easter and summer, we have this lovely long spring break where the village is ours to do as we please…and that goes for the people who live here as well as us seagulls.

The princess is a pretty chilled chick too. She always looks radiant at this time of year. Her beak is *really* yellow, and the little red bit on the end that looks like lipstick is at it's most kissable scarlet. Her plumage is fabulous too, the white feathers pure and shining and fluffy, and the grey bits and black tips on her wings well defined and toned.

I've noticed that she doesn't ever seem to use her wings or fly anywhere anymore. Maybe she works out when I'm off foraging for grub? Whatever it is, she always looks gorgeous to me and I love her, and I could think of no other gull more beautiful or that I'd rather be with.

We spend the lengthening evenings of spring cuddled up close together up in the gullery, me and the princess, looking out over the rooftops of the village and watching all the other gulls courting and billing and cooing. I occasionally swoop out over the main street to the bins at the back of the pub or the Harbour Café to bring us back a take-away, and we sit quietly together, eating and chatting, quite happy with each other's company and at peace in our surroundings.

Then it happens. Every spring the same.

The princess seems to get a little more sleepy day by day, around about the time when I can hear people singing the May Day song, '…in the merry morning of May…', every year it's the same. She sleeps all night, wakes for a short time at dawn, then snoozes off again until lunchtime. I'll bring her back a nice piece of scampi and some chips or something from the Harbour Cafe, and she'll smile and maybe eat a little, then fall back asleep again.

Love her as I do, it gets a bit boring with no one to squawk to.

So to amuse myself, I set out to make the gullery a little more comfortable for us both. I go to bushes and pull out small twigs and leaves and stuff, I go to the beach and pick up bits of seaweed, I even bring back bits of coloured string and plastic and empty crisp bags to the gullery, where I dump them on the roof in no particular order.

You think I'm building a nest, don't you?

Well, you *could* be right. It's not a nice neat nest like a robin or blackbird might build, all cute and homely and full of down and feathers and fluff, nor is it a big, clever, well constructed thing like a rook or crow might make, with all interlocking twigs and sticks in a nice round bowl shape.

No. Mine is more…er…a pile of old twigs and seaweed and junk dumped in a heap up in the gullery.

You think I'm building a nest don't you?

The princess likes it though. She, when she eventually wakes up, waddles across from the bare slates where she has been sitting sleeping and plonks herself right down on the pile of old twigs and sticks and seaweed and junk (should we call it the nest?) and settles down for another snooze. She seems very comfortable with what I do for her, and starts to sleep even longer.

'Yawn, yawn….Zzzz…Snore, snore…' It really is a bit boring without her to squawk to.

Then, all of a sudden, everything falls into place. The lovey-dovey cuddles and courting, the tiredness and the sleeping and yawning and snoring and zzzing, the twigs and sticks and stringy stuff, the time of year, the spring fever…I suddenly remembered; it always happens the same way…

Eggs!

No, I don't mean poached or fried or boiled, or scrambled eggs on toast, sunny side up or over easy with muffins, or one of those great big sweetie filled chocolate eggs in a box and shiny wrapper you can get at Easter, although I would gladly eat one of them if anybody were foolish enough to leave one lying about.

I mean *seagull* eggs.

Twins this year! Two bonny green eggs with cute brown blotches…sweet! Oh, she always has beautiful eggs, the princess. Beautiful, just like her.

I looked at her and she was blooming…blooming gorgeous that gull. She looked back at me and smiled her serene smile. Mother of my eggs…she's divine, she is. She's the only gull for me, she's the most beautiful gull in the world, my gull, she makes me want to sing with happiness!

I moved a little closer to have a good look at the twins…

She pecked me hard, right on the side of the neck…nasty, spiteful, vicious creature that she is…there was no need for that, no need at all! I only wanted a closer look at your stupid eggs!

No. I mustn't overreact. It must have been an accident. Perhaps, in her tiredness, she thought I was a magpie. Yes, that must have been it. She thought that I was a magpie who was going to steal one of the eggs! How silly. I leaned forward again slowly and peeped. There they were, the twins, a lovely shape and…ouch!! This time she pecked me even harder, on the back of the head! Temper, temper, princess!

Then I remembered. The princess always gets a bit tetchy when she's sitting on eggs. Last year, as I recall, she yanked out a couple of my tail feathers in her rage, and the year before she grabbed me by the webbed foot and made me squawk in agony. Oh yes, I love her, but she can be a funny gull at times.

Nasty, spiteful, vicious creature!

So I just spent the next few weeks flying back and forth, to and fro the Harbour Café's bins, bringing back all her favourite food whilst she sat on the eggs, and if I dropped it too close to her or the twins she'd squawk or peck or flap her wings at me, just like I was some nuisance that needed to be shooed away!

Me, a nuisance, can you believe it? Me! I was doing my best. If you ask me, she's a bit of an ungrateful gull at times.

And all the time, the twins didn't move, they just lay there side by side under the downy feathers of the princess' lovely white warm tummy. Before they came along, when it was just me and the princess all cuddled up all lovey-dovey, that's where I used to like to be…

Still, it was mostly a happy event, and the twins were pretty well behaved, not rolling around or wriggling or making any sort of din, not like some eggs you hear about, and maybe we should have made the most of it, the princess and me, instead of arguing and bickering and pecking and squawking so.

We knew that it could not go on forever, and that something had to happen. We just couldn't remember what. Then, firstly a small hole in the shell, then a crack, then an opening, and then…

Chicks!

Chicks!

Ok, now I know its hard to tell boys from gulls (ha, ha! Boys from *gulls*!). They all look the same to you, don't they? Well, there are certain differences I can tell you, and as a seagull of the same species, you just know deep down what they are. It's a bit like when I drop the twigs and sticks and junk and stuff all over the roof in a sad attempt to make a nest. It's *instinct*, that's the word, instinct.

My instinct told me that the two little browny-downy bouncing baby balls of fluff with big flappy webbed feet and ever-open beaks were boys. Twin boys! I couldn't believe our luck.

After a great deal of thought, the princess (who was in a slightly better mood by now) and I decided on their names. Clarence and Claude.

What? What!!? What is wrong with Clarence and Claude? How very rude of you! They are lovely names.

And guess what? Within days they were big, monstrous, monster, browny-downy balls of fluff, with huge, flappy webbed feet like flippers, and gawpy, ever-open beaks that squealed and squawked and squeaked from dawn to dusk for food and food and more food, and then can you believe it, even more food.

Now, as you know, I pride myself on the way I can get hold of food no matter what. It's what I do, right? I'm a gull.

Well, Clarence and Claude had appetites like no other chicks we'd ever had before, and the princess (who was by now back on the wing, thank heaven) and I were starting to get a little exhausted at their constant demands for feeding. It wasn't that they both had huge appetites, although Claude certainly did and would eat anything we brought him and more, but Clarence was *fussy*.

Now fussy eaters are a problem. You could bring back a raw cod's head from the fish cellars and a few chips from out the back of the take away for Claude and he'd whooph the lot down in one or two gulps. Head back, swallow, gone! Give the same to Clarence, and he'd maybe pick an eye out of the cod, and a bit of the lip or something, then he'd turn his beak up at the rest and sit there looking all sulky and miserable.

Claude with a light snack! Clarence, however, was a fussy eater...

Clarence seemed to be content to sit and preen his downy feathers for hours at a time. He would wash his beak in a small puddle on the roof until it was shiny and clean. He would walk over with his flappy flippers to a roof skylight window and gaze at his own reflection for a whole morning, occasionally tapping the glass with his beak, and holding his head to one side, then the other. One day, he even borrowed his mother's fishbone tiara and put it on his head and gazed at himself for hours as if *he* were the princess. I was beginning to get a little concerned about our Clarence…

These things were made all the worse by the fact that all the other couples up in the gullery seemed to have had chicks as well. Everywhere you looked up, every rooftop, every gutter, every chimney pot, every single slate and tile it seemed had a big, browny-downy, fluffy, flapper-footed, squawking, squeaking chick on it, and they all seemed to be as greedy as Claude.

The demands for food for hundreds of chicks became overwhelming. Not a dustbin was unravaged, not a take away wrapper left unopened, no fish box was unturned or bin liner left unripped or unexplored. No street was left uncovered in garbage, no rooftop was without its larder of chick food.

15

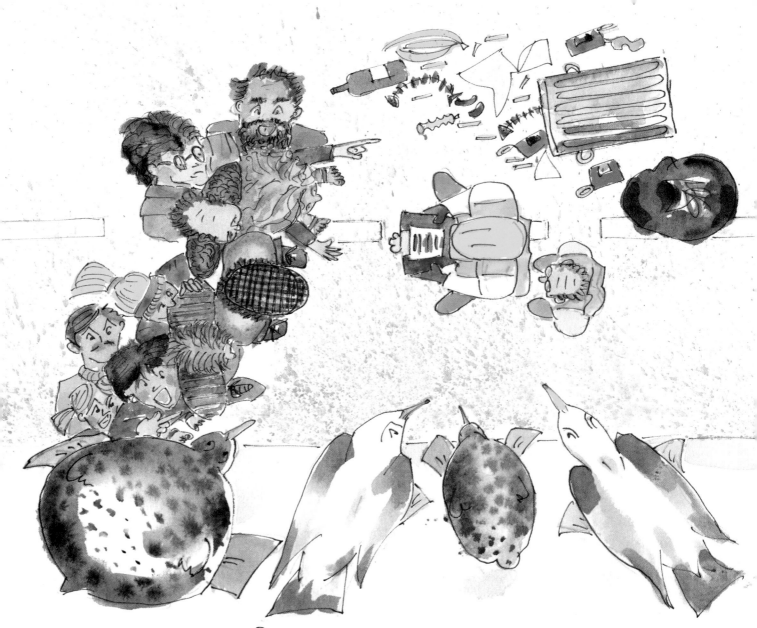

The man from the council and the
angry crowd...a gull's eye view.

No small child was safe with it's ice cream, no old granny with her cream tea, no one anywhere could be sure that their nasty pasty wouldn't be snatched by gulls desperate to feed their ever demanding, squealing, squeaking, squawking squabs.

Then came the man from the council.

I knew that he was from the council because he had a silly little badge with his photo on it, in a clear plastic case on a string around his neck. He wore a white all-in-one disposable suit and a facemask over his mouth and nostrils. He carried a clipboard and biro. He wore Wellington boots. Green ones. Over his boiler suit he wore a fluorescent green jerkin bearing the words 'pest control'. And on his head he wore a bright yellow safety helmet....

Pest control indeed!

That safety helmet was a very sensible item.

Followed by a crowd of people, the man from the council began to walk around the village streets. Every so often, he would stop and one of them would point up at the rooftops and he would write something down with his biro.

He took photographs of the rubbish in the street and of the chicks and the sticks and twigs and stuff up in the gullery. He took photographs of the bin liners and bins and take away wrappers, and he took photographs of me and the princess and the other gulls.

The man from the council pulled some notices out from inside his jacket. He handed them to another man, his helper Jasper, who began to pin them onto the telephone poles along the street. I leaned forward and read one of them. It made me very cross.

It said *'The herring gull is a pest that carries diseases and spreads germs. It litters the area and encourages other vermin such as rats and mice. Do not feed them. Keep rubbish in bins with secured lids.*
By order: North Cornwall Council.'

Blooming cheek! Pest! Diseases! Spreading germs!! Vermin! Rats and…oh never mind. How are we supposed to feed all the fluffy, flapper-footed, squealing, squawking squabs if you keep all our grub in bins with proper lids on, eh? Hang on matey, you can't do that, we're protected! There's hundreds of chicks around here and that could starve them all!

I turned to the princess and Clarence and Claude to ask what they thought. It was then that I noticed that Clarence was missing. Oh my lord, turn your back for five minutes eh? I peered over the edge of the guttering.

The crowd of people had all gathered around Mrs Baker's doorway, and the man from the council was in front of them all. They were looking down at the step. They stood back as the man from the council bent over and reached out his hands. He was by now wearing a pair of disposable rubber gloves.

Clarence was down in Mrs Baker's doorway, admiring his reflection in the clean glass of her door. He was finishing off an iced bun sprinkled with hundreds and thousands and with a small cherry on top. Mrs Baker had put it out for him on the step on a pretty plate with a paper doily when she had realised that Clarence had fallen down from the gullery. Clarence leaned forward and plucked the cherry and swallowed it whole.

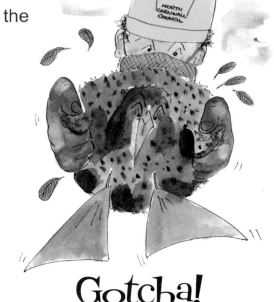

'Right, gotcha!' laughed the man from the council as he grabbed poor Clarence from behind.

'And you,' he said gruffly to poor, kind Mrs Baker, 'leave off feeding 'em unless you want to end up in court.'

'Yeah, leave off you old bat!' said someone else.

Gotcha!

'Yeah, they're vermin!'

I watched poor Clarence struggling and writhing and grabbing at the man from the council's rubbery finger with his little beak. It was a forlorn struggle.

'Right, lets get you to the cage. We'll take you to the bird pound with all the other strays, eh?' he said kindly, loud enough for the crowd to hear, and then added under his breath, 'And, you filthy diseased bag of feathers, if no one claims you there they'll wring your blinking neck…' Clarence looked back at him, and splattt right down the man's disposable all-in-one suit in utter fear. That's my boy…

But I could bear it no more. I leapt from the roof and dived at the man, squawking my loudest, fiercest war squawk. I aimed my beak at the back of his head, just below the yellow helmet…

He must have had eyes in the back of his head.

'Umbrella Jasper!' he shouted, and from nowhere his sidekick Jasper opened up a large golfing umbrella and held it up over the two of them. I quickly came out of my dive and flew upwards again and landed on the roof above them. As they walked along the street towards the harbour area, I flew from

Umbrella, Jasper!

roof to roof and gutter to gutter, making as loud a to-do as I possibly could. But I couldn't get near them.

I have never heard a worse sound than the sad and fearful squeaking and squealing of poor Clarence, as he was taken to the open rear doors of the pest control van and shoved inside the metal cage.

And they wonder why us gulls get aggressive when we've got young?

The man from the council pulled off his disposable gloves and dropped them into a bin. He plucked a wet wipe from a sachet, and cleaned off the splattt that Clarence had put down his leg.

'You see, Jasper, these wipes have an active germ killing ingredient. Just the job when dealing with filthy creatures like this,' he said, nodding at Clarence who was cowering pathetically in the cage. He took another wipe from a sachet and cleaned off his hands and fingers, over and over again.

'Can't be too careful, Jasper,' he said. 'There could be rotting beak syndrome, or feather fungus, or gullitis. I've heard of a pest control officer who was nipped by a gull and died a most terrible death.'

'No…' gasped Jasper, taking the wet wipe from him and dropping it into the bin.

'Oh yes Jasper, down at St Ives' he said, stepping out of the disposable suit and shoving it into a plastic sack. 'Rabies, Jasper. He was savaged by a giant gull with a beak like a cutlass, and went mad and drowned in his own saliva!'

'No…'

He nodded and handed Jasper the sack. 'Ever heard of the Black Death, Jasper? There are those that say it was seagulls what spread that. Some say that they still carry the spores to this day, and it's only a matter of time…'

Clarence was scratching at the mesh of the cage with his flappy feet.

'Don't you worry, Jasper. At least we've got one of the filthy brutes. Now, all the excitement has brought on hunger pangs. A mug of tea and egg and chips in the Harbour Café is in order, care of North Cornwall council.'

I watched from the roof as the two men walked away from the van and into the café.

It was a short while after that I heard a great commotion from back up the street. There was a hideous chorus, a tumultuous screeching, of squawking and squealing. I saw what could only be described as a slow moving, browny-downy, fluffy, flapper-footed carpet of squeaking squabs moving as one towards the harbour and the Harbour Café. They completely covered the street. There were hundreds of them. And they were intent on revenge.

They were led by a particularly plump and fluffy individual, whose flipper-flapper feet seemed larger than those of the others in his army, a chick from whose beak came the most ear splitting screech that I had ever heard. A screech like that of a banshee…

I am proud to tell you that it was Claude.

The squab squad advances...

Boldly Claude flip-flapped in

At the end of the street, Claude stopped, and peeped around the corner of the doorway of the Harbour Café. Boldly he flip-flapped in, followed by the squealing squab army. The man from the council froze with horror in his seat, his plate of egg and chips in front of him on the table. Jasper, terrified, backed up against the wall. The squealing squabs quickly flooded in and surrounded the man from the council. The Harbour Café was totally full of angry, greedy, seagull chicks.

'Nnnow wait a minute…' said the man.

Claude leapt up onto the table. He dipped his head and stared at the man. Claude looked down at the egg and chips in front of him. He opened his beak and scooped up the fried egg. The man trembled. Claude lifted his head and swallowed the fried egg whole.

That's my boy…

The man from the council couldn't move. His hands gripped the table. He was sweating. His eyes rolled right, then left, up, then down. All he could see was brown fluff and hundreds of nasty, sharp little beaks. He shivered as he thought of all the germs and illness and diseases that might attack him. And all the time a pair of staring eyes were boring into him. Claude's eyes.

Claude dipped his head again and flipped it from side to side on the plate, scattering all the chips onto the floor around the table. The chicks dived in and

grabbed and gobbled up whatever they could, squealing and screeching and squawking.

But Claude had his eyes on an even bigger, tastier morsel.

Claude grabbed the terrified man from the council by the hooter with his beak, and gave it the most almighty twist and tug. But it would not come off, and Claude was disappointed because despite having already eaten the man's egg, he was still rather peckish. He squeezed his beak and tried again but still the nose would not budge and so, sensing that it was probably a waste of time, he jumped down onto the floor and joined in the chip melee down there with all the other squabs instead.

Still the nose would not budge

I took full advantage of the distraction. I flew to the rear of the pest control van, which was still open, and flipped up the catch on the cage door. Hey, if a gull can manage to open a bin liner, then a catch on a cage door is no problem.

Poor Clarence, still squealing and very frightened, jumped out of the van and down onto the road, and ran as fast as his flipper-flappered feet could take him, just as the vast tide of still squealing chicks and his brother Claude left the cafe by the same door like a moving carpet of fluff, back towards the end of the street where we all lived, and away.

No problem!

28

It was a bonus that whilst in the pest control van, I saw a small plastic Tupperware box on the front seat. Clarence being safe now, I guessed that I'd better check it out just in case…

Well, the men from the council certainly have nice packed lunches, and two lots of tuna and mayonnaise sandwiches, a bag of cheese and onion and a Mars bar later, I eventually flew back to the gullery to see that, happily, sanity had returned. All the chicks had somehow got back onto the roofs, and all the council man's posters had been torn down.

But the princess looked at me with sadness in her eyes. Claude regurgitated a chip and ate it again. Clarence was nowhere to be seen.

It was then that from inside her attic, Mrs Baker undid the latch to the roof light window, and reaching up with her gentle old hand passed our chick out and up into the gullery.
'There you go, sweetie,' she said, 'that's a good girl, up you go.'
And as dainty as you like, Clarence hopped off her hand and up onto the roof.

Mrs Baker held up one of the posters for me to see, and then slowly she tore it in half. She passed out four iced buns, all sprinkled in hundreds and thousands and topped with a cherry.
'She likes those, dear,' said Mrs Baker, smiling at me and closing the window.

She? I began to wonder. Clarence picked off the cherry from a cake and ate it and left the rest, and then she walked to the window and stared at her reflection. Left, then right, up, then down. She picked up the fishbone tiara and put it on her head. Beautiful. She was such a pretty gull, just like her mother.

Goodbye Clarence. Hello Clarissa! So much for instinct, eh?

The End

Also available

Three mischievous adventures of the wicked seagull on CD

The range of Gully story books

Visit the website for more details

www.thegullery.co.uk

Or phone The Gullery on 01208 880937

The Author

The creator, author and illustrator
of Gully, Jon Cleave, lives in the
heart of the lovely old Cornish
fishing village of Port Isaac with
his wife Caroline and boys Jakes,
George and Theo.... oh yes, and
hundreds and hundreds
of squealing, squawking,
screaming seagulls!